THE COBB GHOUL

GW00514783

*I would like to thank Carl Salter,
my generous-hearted ghost walks mentor;
Alan Dodson for his superb illustrations;
Joanna Smith and the Black Dog Writing Group;
my publisher, Olivia Daly;
Howard Wright; Julia Jensen;
and Judy Epstein for her enthusiastic
support and encouragement*

THE COBB GHOUL

Lyme Regis Ghost Stories

CHRIS LOVEJOY

© Chris Lovejoy 2020

Illustrations © Alan Dodson
Cover photos © Chris Lovejoy

Design and layout © Olivia Daly
Page ornaments by Gordon Johnson. Reproduced
under licence from www.pixabay.com

All rights reserved. No part of this publication may be reproduced,
stored in a retrieval system, or transmitted, in any form or by any
means, electronic, mechanical, photocopying, recording or otherwise,
without prior permission in writing from the author or publisher.

Published by Olivia Daly, Charmouth, Dorset
www.oliviadaly.com

Printed by Advantage Digital Print, Dorchester
www advantagedigitalprint.com

ISBN 978-0-9563721-3-0

CONTENTS

INTRODUCTION

One summer afternoon in 2009, I was walking down the narrow pathway of Sherborne Lane, basking in the warm sun, when all my senses suddenly became alert, and as if in a dream I heard the sound of guttural accents, the clink of armour and the tramp of booted feet on cobblestones. This all passed in a split second, and then once again I was walking down Sherborne Lane hearing only the cries of the seagulls.

This incident made me curious to learn more of the history of my new hometown of Lyme Regis. Imagine my surprise to learn that the end of Sherborne Lane, where I had been walking that day, was where some of the fiercest fighting took place during the Civil War, when Puritan Lyme was besieged by a Royalist force in an eight-week siege in 1644.

Ghosts can perhaps be seen as echoes of past trauma so severe as to imprint the present, beyond time, demanding recognition of past wrongs, or as a desperate cry for redemption or resolution.

I have tried to stay as true as possible to the historical background from which each story has derived.

Readers can decide for themselves how much or how little to believe… Enjoy!

THE COBB GHOUL

The Cobb is a cold and eerie place on a winter night. The gulls scream as the waves lash against ancient stone walls – the haunts of pirates and smugglers, the scene of so much past skulduggery. Today the aquarium is the largest building on the Cobb. However, at one time there was another building on the same site with an altogether darker purpose. This was the quarantine hospital.

In earlier times many diseases such as cholera and typhoid hit the town. Plague and leprosy were not unknown and during severe epidemics the port would be closed; on occasion the town also would be isolated. Anyone arriving in the port would be placed in the quarantine hospital. Many entered its heavy doors but few departed back to the life they had known. Most left under cover of night in a black sack dropped far out at sea.

One evening a young lad was resting in a boat moored up on the shore, relaxing, enjoying the sun after a morning's fishing. All seemed peaceful. However, a smuggling boat had secretly docked nearby. Spying the young lad, the smugglers seized the opportunity, grabbed him and dragged him off to work as a galley slave in their boat. After keeping him in this cruel predicament for some months, the smugglers noticed the boy was becoming sick, and, panicking, they tossed him overboard.

Fortunately, being a good swimmer and close to shore, he managed to float and swim his way back to the beach in Lyme, where he lay exhausted.

He was found and recognised by locals next morning and his mother was immediately called. This was a blessed day! She was so full of joy and gratitude to see her son again, and although weak, he was still alive. However, her rejoicing was short-lived. When the town officials arrived, recognising the symptoms of disease, and despite the desperate pleading of his distraught mother, they ordered him to be placed in the quarantine hospital.

The boy languished in this new captivity for several months, becoming weaker and weaker. His mother would visit every day to look up at the window where he stood. She sent in food she had prepared with her own hand, but nothing could save him. Eventually he went mad and died.

Pity the plight of the late-returning seaman suddenly confronted by a howling, screaming, ghoulish phantom with clawlike fingernails scraping at the top window in a desperate effort to escape. The last known person to see the Cobb ghoul was a fisherman from a well-known local family in the 1960s. For a month afterwards he lay on his bed trembling, struck dumb, unable to speak a word, and was never able to go to sea again…

THE FERRYBOAT

Looking over Lyme Bay from Gun Cliff on a fine summer day, the casual observer might notice leisure boats of various shapes and sizes moving in and out of the harbour, as well as throngs of holidaymakers on the beaches and in the water. In the winter months the moored boats bob up and down with the tide, but otherwise nothing moves except the occasional fishing trawler setting out in the early morning or returning later with the day's catch.

From this perspective, looking over the bay today, it is hard to imagine that in Elizabethan times, some 500 years ago, Lyme Regis was one of the largest trading ports in the country. Ships were bringing in goods from Africa, North America and the Mediterranean coast, and from Lyme boats were even making the icy journey out to Newfoundland. The Cobb harbour was seething with activity and the port so busy that ships often had to wait at anchor offshore for a slot in the harbour to load or unload.

Ferryboats would take the crew from the ships into the town to enjoy the ale houses and the nightlife on offer, as in any sea port. The ferryboat man would let them know he was ready to depart by calling out 'Ferryboat! Ferryboat! Ferryboat!' in a loud voice.

One day three sailors staggered out of one of the pubs, stumbled down to the beach on hearing the ferryboat man's call, and tumbled into one of the small boats.

Now at the turn of the season there's a particular kind of mist that often descends over the bay. It is very thick and localised. If you are unfortunate enough to be caught inside the mist at sea, it is so dense that sailors used to say you could blink your eyes and not see your eyelids. It is also wet and very cold.

On this particular day the mist suddenly descended as the little boat was halfway to its destination off shore. The boat disappeared from view, leaving its occupants shivering inside. Nobody could see in or out.

Shortly after, as was usual, the mist began to disperse… but the boat was nowhere to be seen.

'This is strange – it's only a short distance across the Bay,' people were saying. 'There's no danger, but something must have happened.'

'Perhaps those drink-sodden sailors got into a fight and capsized the boat,' suggested others, laughing, 'but we will see them again.'

What they meant by this was that, as everybody here in Lyme knows, anything that falls into the sea, be it an old barrel, a dead dog or a body, always sooner or later ends up on Back Beach, below the church. But neither the boatman, nor the three sailors, nor the boat nor any part of it was ever seen again.

However, get up early, just as the last star is disappearing in the early dawn, and come down to Gun Cliff. Listen carefully, and from the rocks below, as many others have before, you may hear the faint sound of a ghostly voice carried on the wind, calling:

'Ferryboat! Ferryboat! Ferryboat!'

Father Joseph

After the river has passed under three bridges on the outskirts of the town, and fed the mill, it disappears beneath a row of houses along Coombe Street. Reappearing briefly, it crosses under Bridge Street before finally flinging itself into the sea.

At one time this was a secret route into town for smugglers delivering goods in the night through trapdoors into the houses above. It was a dark and dangerous passage. A sudden squall or storm at sea could create a backwash, capsizing or crushing the boats against the tunnel walls. Bodies would be found next morning on the foreshore.

This was also the route used by another visitor. Father Joseph was an elderly Catholic priest with a large jaw and intensely bright blue eyes that belied his age. In the wake of Catholic exclusion laws, far from fleeing this intensely puritan, anti-Catholic town, he remained in hiding. He would, he knew, have been hanged or worse if caught here in Lyme.

One bitterly cold winter night, when the stars, like shards of ice, seemed to pierce the grey woollen smock he wore over his clerical robes, the priest approached the tunnel entrance. He looked carefully from side to side then stepped cautiously into his tiny boat. He lit a tallow candle in a jar, crossed himself several times, and started to row upstream.

The house that Father Joseph visited that night belonged to a prominent Puritan merchant who had no idea that his wife, despite all appearances, was a secret adherent of the 'old religion,' as it was called, that he so despised. His frequent absences on business to other towns, however, gave her the opportunity to secretly invite the priest into their house.

On that fateful night, with his few devoted followers surrounding him before the simple makeshift altar, Father Joseph was saying Mass when the meeting was suddenly disturbed by heavy footsteps and the unexpected return of the merchant. The panicked woman desperately tried to distract her husband and hide the evidence, but in vain. When he saw the priest standing there and realised the enormity of his wife's deception, horrified and outraged he grabbed a knife and plunged it into the priest's throat, pulled up the trapdoor and flung him into the river below, then turned towards his wife. Before he could stop her, however, with a loud scream she hurled herself through the open trapdoor, choosing the same fate as her beloved priest.

For many years after, on the anniversary of the murder, occupants of the houses on the street would hear, floating up from the river below, the hypnotic sound of the Latin words of the Mass accompanied by the screams of a drowning man and woman. When the worried residents opened the trapdoors, however, the sounds would cease, only to resume when they were closed again. Furthermore, women washing clothes the next morning in the river below reported that, no matter the original colour they went in, their clothes all came out a bloody red.

Startled witnesses approaching the Lynch at dusk have occasionally glimpsed the phantom figures of a priest with hands folded in front, and a woman in black, silently drifting together above the surface of the water, as if in deep conversation.

THE COBB ALE

Cyril Wanklyn, Lyme's great Edwardian historian, first mentions the Buddle Ghost in his book 'Lyme Regis – a Retrospect': 'When visible, she passed to and fro the Buddle chanting the following refrain:

"I rue the time
I sold water for wine
and combed my hair of a Sunday."

She may or may not have been a victim of Puritan persecution… but she served a useful purpose as a means of frightening naughty children.'

Eight weeks after Easter, since medieval times, Lyme had been celebrating Whitsun with its own unique festival known as the Cobb Ale. Ostensibly to raise funds for the maintenance of the ancient Cobb harbour, it was a carnival of feasting and secular entertainment, joyously anticipated by most of the townsfolk. This year, 1640, however, something was different.

John Trevor, harbourmaster and owner of a local tavern, the Swan, and the foremost 'warden' or organiser of the festival, was perplexed and uneasy as he chatted with fellow seamen and other wardens in the bar that night.

'It's going to be a tough one, to be sure, this year,' he said. 'That humbug Geare is spewing forth like a sea serpent against our project and the likes of us ordinary townsfolk. People are becoming afraid. There's too many fanatics in this town.'

Heads nodded among murmurs of agreement, even as some men

looked nervously over their shoulders towards a group of militiamen standing aloof in one corner.

'I heard he's even got the ear of that old fool the mayor,' Trevor continued unrestrainedly, 'though Lord knows how. He of all people knows how our town benefits from the festival.'

There was a shuffling of feet and a few dark looks in their direction as the militiamen moved outside. For a few moments an uneasy silence enveloped the bar.

The silence was abruptly broken by the entry of a raven-haired young girl of about seventeen calling out 'Sir! Sir! The players have arrived! Mr Lewis is here with the horses.' This was Alice Meeker, the orphaned daughter of a drowned fisherman of the publican's acquaintance. He had taken pity on her and brought her into his household as a servant. She had soon become indispensable, and a deep bond had developed between them – he treated the girl as if she was his own daughter.

The landlord and the girl left together. As they rounded the door into the courtyard, they were greeted by the neighing of horses and shuffling of hooves, mingling with the voices of the new arrivals. The landlord immediately strode up to a ruddy-faced burly man with bushy side whiskers and wearing a yellow waistcoat, and he squeezed his outstretched hand, exclaiming loudly:

'Welcome, Abner! Welcome all! Stables are ready for the horses. First, drink and victuals on the house! Alice will take care of you.'

As Abner Lewis and his troupe of players made their way into the main bar to the cheery greeting of most of the occupants – the players were always a popular part of the festival – another very different meeting was taking place in another part of town.

John Hassard, the mayor, was moving toward the end of his three-term tenure. A wealthy, straightforward freeman of the borough, he had little sympathy with the increasing disharmony and religious conflict in which the town had become embroiled. He disliked the new vicar, whom he regarded as a troublemaker, and resented his presence on his own turf, here in the Guildhall. Why couldn't he confine his activities to St Michael's and the parish, like his predecessors?

On the other side of the oak table, John Geare leaned towards him menacingly. This dark-haired, muscular vicar, with his intense gaze, looked more like a fairground wrestler than a man of the cloth. Now, surrounded by his grim-faced Calvinist followers – some, against all protocol, carrying arms – the vicar spoke slowly and deliberately in a thin, expressionless voice:

'Mayor, you have received many letters and petitions from the church outlining our concerns for the moral health of our citizens and about the festival of immorality and devil-worship being at this very time prepared in this town. Are you now willing to act with us, the true followers of our Lord, or do you rather associate yourself with the forces of Satan, heretics and unbelievers?' Here he paused a moment, then continued, 'Your past family connections with papists, I might add, have been noted.'

Hassard shot to his feet in fury, but knew he was beaten, and as abruptly sat down. He could not deny his early Catholic upbringing or the peril in which that placed him during these dangerous times.

The following morning was the Lord's Day and before his crowded congregation, fulminating with rage and righteousness, Geare threw the whole weight of his invective against the Cobb Ale festival and those who organised and participated in it.

On the Monday morning the proclamation was issued, signed by both civic and church authorities, banning the Cobb Ale and promising harsh penalties for any who attempted to maintain it.

The town cryer bore the message to all parts of the town.

Lewis and his players, used to such situations suddenly arising on their travels, hastily departed, as did other festival incomers.

The next day, a group of Geare loyalists, including some members of the garrison, burst into the Swan and dragged Trevor away. Alice, who was present, screaming in protest and flailing her arms, kicked at the shins of the assailants, but to no avail. When they passed through the door, one militiaman turned back and advanced towards the girl; calling her a 'Devil's whore', he struck her a heavy blow in the face. Through her tears and the stinging pain, Alice swore she would be avenged. She recognised the assailant as one of those furtively standing in the corner that previous night as Trevor discussed the festival plans.

In the following days the loyal servants kept the inn open, although customers were few. Hoping for the return of the master any time, nervously and in hushed voices they expressed their dismay at the turn of events. Alice spent her time trying to gain information on the whereabouts and fate of her adopted father. None of the members of the arresting party she approached seemed to know his final destination, only that he had been delivered to the 'cockmoile' – the town jail – but had been taken elsewhere the following day. The mayor, although expressing sympathy, just shook his head, insisting there was nothing he could do. This was a church matter. She tried to contact Geare himself but was repeatedly rebuffed.

A few days later, rumour arrived with the Dorchester coach that Trevor was being held in the county jail on charges of blasphemy and inciting immorality. The next evening, the coachman himself, although he had not personally been present, brought to the Swan the latest news he had heard of the hanging of a prisoner from Lyme that same morning, along with others, in the town square.

Before she could digest the news – was it true? Could it be someone else? – Alice was approached by a smirking militiaman demanding ale, and she recognised him immediately as the one who had struck her. Without hesitation, turning her back, she went behind the bar and returned a moment later with a pot of water she handed him and which he downed, only to throw up immediately protesting wildly while the girl just stared at him with a look of deep malice. Everyone in those days knew that water was only fit for animals to drink, ale being the most common alternative.

Eli Scrope, the militiaman, was in a fever for a week. Rumours about his sickness started spreading around the town, encouraged by angry family members and fellow soldiers. Alice became more and more isolated; even some of the other servants were looking strangely at her. She became more and more anxious and had taken to combing her hair repetitively in a nervous effort to remain occupied, even at church on the Sabbath, which had been duly noticed. Still no further news or confirmation of the fate of John Trevor had been received.

It was the day after the Sabbath when they came for her, led by the vicar himself, and the charge of witchcraft was formally laid against her.

Bound and helpless, she was taken to the riverbed and cast into the water above Gosling Bridge, for the trial by ordeal. When she briefly floated or her head appeared above the water she was greeted with shrieks of 'Witch!' from the watching crowd on the river bank. Her struggles ceased, she started to sink, and her body was last seen floating below the surface of the river passing through the Buddle into the open sea.

John Trevor, a shadow of his former self, pale and unkempt, staggered into the Swan one morning later in the month. The sheriff in Dorchester had thrown out the case and set him free. He was, however, a changed man, who never recovered from his experiences and his grief on learning of his adopted daughter's fate, for which he blamed himself. He sold the inn and kept himself mainly to himself, passing his time between the graveside of his long-dead wife and the Buddle Bridge, where he was the first to report seeing there the ghost of Alice pacing back and forth, singing her sad song:

'I rue the day I sold water for wine and combed my hair of a Sunday.'

THE DESCENT OF ROBERT JONES

No one rejoiced more in the collapse of Cromwell's Commonwealth and the Restoration of King Charles II than ardent, bloodthirsty Royalist Robert Jones. It was probably more his brutal nature than any religious conviction that made him the leader in the harassment and persecution of the various Puritan groups in Lyme. Families were split up and made destitute, chapels were demolished, dissenting clergy were beaten and imprisoned. From his home, the Great House in Broad Street, Jones laid plots and sent out informers. He hunted his prey night and day. There was one above all others who eluded him and for whom he bore a particular hatred – the Reverend Ames Short, the former vicar of St Michael's.

How the Revd Short must have regretted his early 1660 Restoration sermon, welcoming the new king who, far from being the 'pious Prince' he had imagined, had proved to be – as he now believed – a licentious degenerate, an agent of the Devil, or of the Pope. Now facing imprisonment, hunted by church and civil authorities, Short was in hiding, banned from his parish.

A rustling in the undergrowth and the parting of twigs and brambles announced the arrival of three more men and a woman. The whispered password 'Lamb of God,' grunted greetings and the shuffling of feet followed as the new arrivals took their places. It was a dark night, the waning moon so weak as to cast little light but many shadows. The wind blowing up from the sea was cold and threatening, and the newcomers pulled tighter on their cloaks as they huddled closer together. With every fresh gust of the wind and the shaking of leaves and swaying branches, a nervous shiver rippled through the company. They had good reason to be afraid, for since 1663 the intolerance and cruel persecution they suffered had reached a new peak.

These former parishioners had supported their vicar in rejecting the new doctrines and prayer book, which they considered heretical, and were now assembling in a remote region of the Undercliff they called Mount Sion. This was an area where landslips were frequent and much feared.

There was one last arrival. On hearing the firm, familiar greeting, a buzz of approval and excitement arose among the group. He had come!

As they fell silent, settling into a new sense of wellbeing and security, the newcomer rose to speak, Bible in hand. Ames Short, heavily disguised in rough labouring clothes, started on a familiar theme, confidently proclaiming 'The righteous shall flourish and the wicked be overthrown!' and peppering his sermon with quotes from scripture that came easily to his lips. It was only their physical predicament that restrained listeners from shouting 'Halleluiah!' as his words of comfort, ground in rock-solid faith and conviction, stirred their hearts.

At first the speaker, deep in his fervour, did not notice the ripple of anxiety that greeted the faint bark of a dog. However, when the barking increased, and the sound of voices and the flicker of lighted flares alerted their senses, with practised agility the whole company arose as one and fled.

Suddenly there was pandemonium as Jones's bloodhounds crashed through the undergrowth and the shouts of the approaching mob

were heard, spurred on by Jones with loud and angry oaths. A few unfortunates were immediately dragged to the ground by the dogs and mauled, suffering terrible injuries, only to be further assaulted by the pursuing mob. Survivors were tethered, beaten and dragged to the town jail to be interrogated and to be brought before the mayor, a close friend of Jones, the following week.

Among those fleeing was a young woman named Rebecca, who accompanied by her two fisherman brothers was among these last arrivals. Having spent most of their childhood playing in these woods, they were confident of escaping down to the beach. The boys pushed ahead to clear a path, but Rebecca, following close behind, caught her foot in a tree root and tumbled over. As she struggled to free herself, she soon realised her ankle was broken and collapsed to the ground in great distress.

In later testimony before the magistrates, Rebecca described what happened next, and her miraculous deliverance:

'I was lying there helpless when I felt the hot breath of a dog above me and heard a shout of triumph, followed by a string of blasphemous oaths. I immediately recognised the voice as that of our great enemy Captain Jones. In that same moment, a bright flash of lightning revealed to me the leering face of my assailant, leaning over me, ready to strike. Expecting the blow that was to come, I was surprised by a terrible crash, like the end of the world, and heard the rumbling of falling rocks and the ground shaking beneath me. I opened my eyes as the noise continued and found myself on the edge of a huge gulf. A chasm had appeared just before where I lay, and almost immediately I heard a terrible scream – I swear I caught a glimpse of thin hairy arms and the claws of demons dragging the blasphemer down into the new-formed abyss. As the rumbling and screams became fainter, I heard a dog whimpering, although it ran off before I could offer some comfort to the dumb beast. My thoughts then turned to my brothers Aaron and Joseph and whether they had survived the slippage. I was overwhelmed with gratitude when they came to my rescue the next morning as I don't know that I could have survived another night out there alone and in such discomfort.'

A few days later, a returning sea captain and his crew told the story in the Ship Inn of how just off the Scilly Isles they had seen a strange black barque looming out of the fog with what appeared to be demons astride a large black coffin. When hailed with the traditional greeting, 'Where bound? What cargo?' a cold eerie voice replied, 'To deliver the doomed soul of Robert Jones from Lyme Regis to Hades!' As the fog lifted, no further sight of the ghostly vessel was to be seen.

Historical note: Ames Short continued preaching and supporting his followers to the frustration of his own father, a landed gentleman, who cut him out of his will. He suffered several periods of imprisonment and, though often destitute, survived. With the passing of the Act of Indulgence in 1672, his condition improved as he was legally entitled to preach again under strict licence. His last period of imprisonment ended with the arrival of William of Orange and the Act of Tolerance of 1689, which granted freedom of worship to non-conformists.

MONMOUTH & THE
HANGING JUDGE

In 1685 the King of England was James II, and he was a Catholic. He was not much liked in Lyme, which from early times had been a very Puritan town. Indeed, his popularity in most of the mainly Protestant country was low as he tried to bring more Catholics into prominent positions. James had a nephew, the Duke of Monmouth, who was the illegitimate son of the previous king, Charles II. Monmouth, a Protestant, was in exile in Holland for suspected involvement in a previous rebellion.

It was a fine clear morning on June 11th when alarmed onlookers on the cliffs observed three heavily armed warships approaching the shore, west of the Cobb. The Duke of Monmouth, in a foolhardy, ill-prepared attempt to usurp the throne from his uncle, had landed, to the applause of most of the local population. Less than a month later, however, after wandering the west of England in a futile attempt to gather the necessary support, he was forced to abandon his dream of becoming king after a disastrous defeat at the battle of Sedgemoor. It took five strokes of the axe to remove his head at the Tower of London.

A furious king unleashed a terrible revenge. His Lord Chief Justice, Judge Jeffries, began what became known as the 'Bloody Assizes', sweeping through the West Country with his own unique brand of justice. In the words of Lyme historian Cyril Wanklyn, 'A great and bitter cry arose on every side.'

Jeffries was a terrible man who took sadistic pride in executing

'traitors' in the most barbarous manner – unless, of course, extortionate bribes were paid. A drunkard, suffering kidney stones and gout, he would stand up in court, slowly look around menacingly at the terrified prisoners and exclaim in a loud voice, 'I can smell Protestants!' before roughly thrusting himself down.

To save time it was announced in advance that those who pleaded innocent could expect to be hanged, drawn and quartered if (inevitably) they were found guilty, while those who pleaded guilty could expect (on payment of the customary bribe) nothing worse than a lifetime detention as a slave on a Caribbean plantation, or a simpler execution.

Twelve men from Lyme Regis were hanged, drawn and quartered on the beach where Monmouth landed, while Jeffries, it was rumoured, was dining in the Great House in Broad Street with the mayor of Lyme Regis. The bloody heads of the unfortunate victims were impaled on the front railings, much, no doubt, to his great satisfaction.

Jeffries' fortunes, however, fell three years later with the ascent of the Dutch Protestant William of Orange to the throne and the flight and exile of James. The 'Hanging Judge', now a very sick man, was captured and condemned, and died himself alone in the Tower.

It was the evening of the anniversary of Jeffries' death. The mayor of Lyme – a royal supporter at that time, of course – was enjoying dinner with his guests at the Great House in Broad Street when the meal was disturbed by a strange scraping sound coming from the upper floor. Fearing rats or other vermin, three younger family members leapt up from the table to investigate.

A moment later there was a terrified scream and the three came tumbling down the stairs one on top of the other, as if there had been a terrible accident. White-faced and trembling, they stutteringly explained to the amazed gathering what they had seen. It was none other than the ghastly figure of Jeffries himself. He was wearing the ceremonial black cap of death, and was dressed in his robes and gown, shuffling through the corridors and muttering in his distinctive hoarse voice, 'Guilty! Guilty!' and in one hand shaking a bloody bone.

Later, when others tentatively mounted the stairs to check further, they reported no trace of the horrible spectre. However, all remarked on a nauseating smell of burning flesh and alcohol, which lingered, people said, for several months, and could even be picked up by sensitively nosed people years later.

Incidentally, the Great House is now Boots the Chemist.

Maggie Wylde

In 1685 some thirty per cent of Lyme's male population joined the Monmouth Rebellion. In the wake of the Bloody Assizes that followed its failure, the king's spies were everywhere, and the town was in terror and turmoil. People were being accused, arrested, executed. Many whole families fled and the population of Lyme plummeted to its lowest level since the Medieval period.

Maggie Wylde, or 'Mad Mag' as she was popularly known, was a cheerful, simple young girl of erratic speech and behaviour, generally regarded as a bit crazy but harmless, who lived with her elderly grandmother on the edge of town and did menial chores for neighbouring households. She was just sixteen when Monmouth marched into Lyme and she was immediately taken with his strikingly handsome features, plumed hat, fancy clothes and commanding presence. Wherever Monmouth went, Maggie followed, yelling out at the top of her voice, 'Long live King Monmouth! God save King Monmouth!'

After Monmouth's dreams were shattered at the Battle of Sedgemoor, people remembered, and Maggie among many others was arrested and put in the jail. Every market day she would be taken out and placed in the stocks, and cruel, idle people would torment her and throw things at her. The poor girl, who secretly believed her absent imagined lover would come and rescue her, could not live long with this kind of treatment.

After her cruel death, people crossing George's Square at night, in front of the inn where Monmouth had first stayed, recounted how on entering the square they heard a high-pitched female voice calling, 'Monmouth! Oh Monmouth! Where are you? Tarry not! Come to me, beloved!'

This outburst would be followed a few seconds later by the clatter of hooves and the sudden appearance of a huge black charger. Seated upon on it was the Duke of Monmouth himself, with one arm raised as if waving to cheering crowds, while under his other arm he was carrying his bloody head.

Later, other witnesses described how as the duke was passing, they caught the fleeting glimpse of a ghostly pale young girl, looking down from an upstairs window of Monmouth House, waving and beckoning enthusiastically.

Still others described being accosted by a dishevelled barefooted old woman in George's Square, dressed in rags and calling out in a strange, aggressive accent, while pointing at them with a withered finger, 'Where is he? Where's Monmouth? Tell me! You saw him!'

The spectre would then suddenly disappear with a chilling scream. Such people declared that after witnessing this incident their lives were never the same again.

In truth, such was the trauma of the failed rebellion in this town that for years afterwards many people refused to believe Monmouth was dead, claiming he had escaped and a criminal had been executed in his place.

LITTLE GIPSY ROSE

No. 13 The Gables, on the other side of the road to St Michael's Church, was opened as Lyme's cottage hospital in 1897. It had an operating theatre designed by Lord Lister, he of antiseptic fame. The Lister family was prominent in Lyme in the early years of the twentieth century.

At one time, every season there was a gypsy encampment on Timber Hill above the Charmouth Road. Young girls used to come down from the camp and sell flowers outside the hospital to visitors.

One particular season there was often to be found a bright, sweet-natured girl of about eight years of age in front of the hospital selling her flowers. Known as Little Rose, she was popular with the sick patients' visitors and relatives, who were happy to buy her colourful bouquets. However, that year there was a tragic accident which cost the poor child her life. She was playing in the road nearby when a horse bolted with a carriage and trapped her under the wheels. The family came and took her away and from that time onwards there was never another gipsy encampment on Timber Hill.

Some time later a young man was visiting his mother in the hospital. She was very sick.

'Son,' she said to him as he settled by her bedside, 'who was that sweet little girl who brought me violets and spoke to me words of such kindness and comfort?'

The young man, seeing no violets beside her, and knowing how ill his mother had been, thought she was probably dreaming and didn't give it much attention. That night, however, she died.

On the morrow when he returned, he became curious thinking these were among his mother's last words. So, he approached one of the nurses and started to say, 'Last night my mother mentioned something about a young girl who brought her violets and…'

'Ah yes,' the nurse interrupted. 'We've never seen her but many of our patients, always shortly before they pass over, tell us about a little girl who comes to comfort them and brings them violets…'

A little light diversion

Many years later, a very sick elderly gentleman was lying in bed in the hospital. Machines around him were connected to a tangle of drips and tubes. His wife and only daughter were at his bedside. His daughter suddenly noticed her father looking at her very intently and clearly struggling to communicate something, but the words were not coming.

Ooh, the young girl thought, Daddy must have a special message, just for me! She leant closer and closer to try and catch his meaning, but as he struggled she noticed his face was starting to go blue. Fearing the worst, she grabbed a paper and pencil from the bedside and thrust it under his hand and he frantically started scribbling, until suddenly there was a large gasp… and his head fell back for the last time. Desperate to see Daddy's last message, the girl grabbed the paper and read:

'Get off the bed, you're sitting on my oxygen!'

THE HEADLESS SOLDIER

A pale moon winked conspiratorially through the misty sky as Sam Hodder trudged his way home after a long day's toil in the shipyard and his customary stopover at the Ship Inn. He was smiling at a joke he'd shared with a friend, and was looking forward to his dinner when, mounting the ancient steps beside the church, he suddenly stopped short, just preventing himself from tripping over a hard sack-like object. Cursing, he bent over to examine it, and was shocked to see the body of a soldier lying there. The head, however, was missing.

After he had raised the alarm, people gathered, some asking, 'Has anyone seen a soldier here in Lyme?'

'We know plenty of sailors,' others replied, 'but we've not seen no soldier here in Lyme.'

As nobody could identify the victim, they took the body to the vicar at St Michael's, who after due consideration arranged for a burial in the paupers' area at one end of the graveyard.

Now at that time there was a room on the top floor of the old Monmouth Hotel, opposite St Michael's, that had the reputation of being the most haunted room in Lyme Regis. Its reputation was such that people would pay money to try and persuade their friends to spend the night there, but none succeeded.

At regular intervals during the night they would hear, coming as if from inside the walls, the sound of horses neighing, of carriage wheels approaching, running footsteps, screams and the firing of muskets. In the interval there would be a sudden cracking sound like the dropping of a large object.

The few who stayed longer described how, around midnight, the grandfather clock in the corner would suddenly chime wildly. The dials would start whirling rapidly around the clock face, until the door of the clock snapped open, revealing not a pendulum but the body of a hanged man, face hideously distorted, rope around his neck, swinging from side to side.

Others described how the bed slowly rose from the ground and started shaking vigorously. Most fled screaming long before.

That room was eventually locked up and abandoned.

One day the proprietor of the Monmouth Hotel noticed there was something wrong with the roof. Those blasted seagulls must be nesting up there again, he thought, and he hired a thatcher to go up and repair it.

Following his instructions, the thatcher went up through the eaves to locate the problem and he was just above that notorious room when he found his way barred by a false wall. Surprised, he broke a way through, and entering the tiny alcove on the other side he saw in one corner, covered in cobwebs, an old metal casket.

Aha, treasure! was his immediate thought. With the utmost care he hid the box in his clothing and secretly carried it home. There, with hammer and chisel he and his wife set about forcing the lock. Eventually they got it open, but to their horror and surprise – and considerable disappointment – they found not gold but a human skull inside a soldier's helmet.

They took their gruesome find over to the vicar who, remembering the headless corpse he'd buried some years before, decided to reinter the body with the head in place.

From that time onwards, the disturbances in that room in the Old Monmouth ceased and in fact it gained the reputation as being one of the most peaceful rooms in Lyme, such that, as a guest once remarked, you could have the sleep of the dead there.

THE VAMPIRE

In the Middle Ages leprosy was a common scourge throughout the country, and leper houses and hospitals were established by the church to care for the victims' spiritual and temporal needs. The Leper Well beside the Lynch is what remains of the leper hospital in Lyme where people who were sick and dying of this and other diseases were isolated under the care and supervision of monks from Sherborne Abbey.

Some years after the final spasm in 1350 of the Black Death, rumours were heard as far away as London and Winchester of a vampire infestation in the West. Several of the undead had apparently been caught, executed, and buried with stakes through the heart in the counties around Dorset.

The church sent out inquisitors far and wide and bishops gave sermons urging vigilance, but the source remained unknown.

Father Ignatius was a well-respected teacher and parish priest, and although regarded as rather severe and aloof, was well known for his learning and charitable works. He was often to be seen visiting the sick at the leper hospital during daylight hours. It was only later that his nocturnal visits and their dreadful purpose were revealed.

If he had been able to confine his habit to the leper hospital and the already dying, perhaps he would have remained undiscovered, but several times a month, needing a supply of fresh nourishment, he would move as far away as possible to select a healthy victim. This person would then, of course, survive as a vampire themselves.

Father Ignatius was passing the market one spring morning when the sister of one of his students approached him from behind a barrow with a big smile, offering him some carrots and holding up a large sprig of garlic. To her amazement the priest flung up his arms, and with wild-eyed fury issued a terrible oath, stumbling away as if in a drunken stupor. The girl stood frozen with shock and disbelief. Later, when she visited her father – an officer in the militia – she told him what had happened that morning.

Her father, aware of the dark rumours, on mention of the garlic became immediately suspicious. He buckled his sword and side dagger into his tunic and, together with the mayor, a curate and another militiaman, rushed off to confront the suspect.

As they burst into his chamber, Father Ignatius greeted them cordially, expressing surprise at such a brusque intrusion. Seeing the girl, he apologised profusely for his earlier behaviour, which he blamed on an ague he had caught during one of his charitable visits to the hospital.

But when the curate pulled out the cross from under his surplice, held it high and started to sprinkle holy water, Father Ignatius leapt forward with an oath. Before they could restrain him, he knocked the girl to the ground and bit deeply into her neck. Her father immediately stuck the dagger into his back, and hesitating only a moment on seeing the horrified pleading look on her face, thrust his sword through his daughter's chest.

Later, one terrified patient of the leper hospital described in evidence to the coroner how the dark-shrouded priest would come in the night to seek out the most severely sick patient and feast on them, leaving them lifeless before hurrying off in the dawn, blood dribbling from his mouth.

Ignatius and the poor girl, his last victim, were buried secretly, as was the custom, in lead-lined coffins with stakes through the heart. The distraught father left immediately for the Holy Land and was never heard of again.

THE LITTLE MERMAID

*The Tudor House in Church Street is a fine example of the old
Elizabethan and Jacobean merchant houses, with a long and varied
history. It is rare in Lyme in having a large well in the cellar. In the
sixteenth century, George Somers, Raleigh and other prominent
seafarers, along with their families, might have dined here and
discussed trade and discoveries in the New World with their wealthy
hosts. Passages discovered in the nineteenth century running from
the cellar to the sea also indicate the house's role in the popular Lyme
pastime of smuggling. This story, however, starts in the seventeenth
century, after the Civil War and the famous Siege of Lyme, when a
strict Puritan interpretation of scripture and morality was the norm.*

The occupants of the house at this time – a proud but pious
merchant and his family, who strived hard to reconcile the
ways of God and Mammon – routinely entertained an itinerant
preacher on his visits to the town.

Meantime, Constance, a young serving girl who had recently
been hired by the family, had with the help of other sympathetic
members of the household staff been struggling to hide a dangerous
secret, which in other circumstances might have been a cause of
great happiness. She was pregnant, a fact that was difficult enough
to conceal before the birth, but upon arrival the baby girl was
becoming more and more difficult to hide.

Upon eventual discovery, the mother, holding her baby, was

summoned before her outraged employers. Sternly rebuked for her moral lapses, and despite the desperate nature of her situation and threatened destitution, Constance was summarily dismissed.

As the girl turned in tears, the preacher, who was present on one of his visits and had been startled by the noise, entered the room. Shocked, he stopped and stood in front of the girl, blocking her exit. As he focused on the baby, and seeing the tiny feet kicking in front of him, his face suddenly darkened. Loosening the covering cloth, he grabbed one foot.

'Yes, it is as I thought!' he exclaimed roughly, as his grip tightened. 'This child has only four toes! This is the Devil's work!'

To the amazement of his hosts, and despite the girl's screams and protests, he grabbed the baby from her grasp, rushed downstairs locking the cellar door behind him, and plunged it into the well.

Many generations later, a new family was living in the house. The children loved exploring and playing in its many ancient rooms, most especially below stairs in the spacious cellar, with its charming, ancient well. One day when they were down below, they heard a giggling sound coming from the direction of the well behind them.

As they looked round over their shoulders, they were astonished to see a tiny mermaid child seated on the low wall surrounding the well. She beckoned them to follow her before turning and diving down inside the well. Of course, the children, amazed by what they saw, were unable and unwilling to follow.

Having realised the children would not follow her, but wanting to share their company, over the next few months the little mermaid would appear frequently, sitting, cooing and giggling on the edge of the well, watching as they played, participating in her own way.

The children became so used to her visits that they came to

accept and even ignore her, agreeing among themselves not to tell the adults, who would of course be angry and accuse them of lying.

However, they grew careless, and one day they came down to play with a new friend, who was so alarmed when the little mermaid unexpectedly appeared that he ran off to tell his parents.

Upon the stern approach of the adults, as their footsteps rang out on the steps outside the cellar door, the tiny mermaid immediately dived back into the well from her accustomed place on the wall, and never appeared again.

THESPIAN RIVALS

Gilbert and Amos were two brothers born in Lyme Regis who both became actors. Gilbert, the elder, was a tall impressive figure with a wide-open face, which he could twist and contort like a rubber mask to imitate any emotional expression or character he chose. He was handsome in an unconventional sort of way, cheerful and outgoing, and a huge hit at parties with the local girls, whom he would entertain with his charm and mimicry.

Amos was also tall, but a sallow, somewhat awkward young man, who lacked his elder brother's charm and ease of manner. He was frequently praised for his perseverance and determination. As the younger child, Amos had always accepted his brother's leadership and indeed for many years had hero-worshipped him. It had seemed only natural that Amos should follow Gilbert into the theatre.

Working in the same company, despite his ability to learn and remember lines and details of staging far better than his brother, Amos noticed, however, that he was continually being cast as a minor character to Gilbert's starring roles. Secretly fiercely ambitious, he began to dwell on this and started becoming more and more bitter. He started to blame his brother for his lowly status and eventually, eaten up with jealousy and frustration, decided that if his career was to take off Gilbert's had to come to an end.

One day Amos invited his brother out on a fishing trip, just the two of them, like when they were young boys. Gilbert was delighted. He had noticed and been troubled by the recent tensions in his brother and half suspected the problem. Out in the boat, in a more relaxed environment, he hoped he would be able to reconnect with him and give him some brotherly advice.

Amos proceeded to hire a small boat, and in the bottom he hid an old anchor. It was a fine day when they set out and Gilbert was relieved to find his brother unusually cheery. However, when they were some way out in the bay, Amos suddenly grabbed the concealed anchor and struck his horrified brother on the head with it before throwing him overboard. Although as he rowed rapidly away Amos could hear his brother's terrified screams and cries for help, he ignored them, stopping only when close to shore to wash away the bloodstains before returning the boat.

No explanation could be found for Gilbert's sudden disappearance, and Amos's career did indeed take off in Gilbert's absence. He became a well-respected actor, especially for his playing of Shakespeare villains. Critics were impressed with his fiery intensity, which seemed to draw out the characters' unforeseen depths of depravity and duplicity. In time he became nationally known and admired, if not particularly well liked by his peers and others who knew him.

After many years and several previously declined invitations, Amos returned to the town of his birth to perform to a packed audience at the newly opened Marine Theatre. The performance was punctuated by gasps of horror and fainting as Amos, alone on stage, presented in turn his most famous roles. After many curtain calls he signed autographs, shook hands, chatted politely and eventually retired exhausted to his dressing room, where he fell asleep.

He woke up after a terrible dream, in which he had seen the bloody anchor and heard again his brother's screams and pleas for help. He suddenly realised he was alone and that everybody else had left the theatre. He made his way to the exit, but was surprised to find the door was locked. He was looking around for another exit when suddenly all the lights went out and the theatre was plunged into darkness. Feeling a sudden panic, he groped his way back towards the stage where a single pale light began to glow.

Suddenly, there on stage and illuminated by the faint flickering, he saw the ghostly figure of his brother Gilbert pointing straight at him. He then found himself seized by unseen hands and pushed into a chair, from where he was forced to witness again and again the re-enactment of his brother's murder by phantom actors.

When people arrived to remind Amos of the celebratory dinner he had been invited to attend with the mayor and other dignitaries, they were surprised to find the theatre closed, and no sign of the great man at his hotel either.

It wasn't until the next morning when the cleaners arrived that they found the body swinging from a rope above the stage with a contorted, terrified expression on its face.

THE CURSE OF
LIZZIE LANGTON

The Angel Inn, at the foot of Mill Lane, until recently lay boarded up and abandoned. The only trace of better times, glimpsed dimly through the window, was the faded notice of a darts competition, which probably never happened. What passing tourist would have guessed that in the early years of the last century the Angel was one of the most popular pubs in Dorset?

The cheery, larger-than-life landlord, Herbert Langton, and his wife Ida ran an establishment renowned for its good beer and friendly service. Their daughter Lizzie was born at the pub. She grew up loving the vibrant atmosphere and the friendly faces that surrounded her, as well as the attention of her doting parents. Her childhood was full of happy memories.

In 1918, however, tragedy struck. After a short, intense struggle, Herbert became a victim of the great influenza epidemic of that year. His wife, after a brief period struggling with her grief and loss, determined to keep the pub going, especially for her daughter, but the pressure proved too much. Ida also died within a few years from exhaustion and a broken heart.

Lizzie, now a young woman suddenly tragically alone, was determined to honour the sacrifices of her much-loved parents, and decided to take over the business herself. However, the economic climate was rapidly changing as the Great Depression settled over the whole country. Profits halved and halved again.

Soon Lizzie was facing bankruptcy and knew she would have to leave the only home she had ever known, full of all her childhood memories as well as the cherished memory of her beloved parents.

On the final day, slowly and deliberately walking through the bars for a last time, with a cry of anguish she threw out her hands, and uttered these fateful words: 'Let no one who comes after me be successful here where I have known such failure! Let no one who comes after me here have good fortune where I have known such misfortune!'

She then closed the door for the last time and walked out without a look behind. No one knows exactly what happened to her after she left the town, but it was rumoured that she died by her own hand the following year.

Two years later, an enterprising young couple decided to reopen the pub. The economy was improving now and the gloom was lifting. This new couple were hardworking and soon the Angel was reviving. Old customers were returning. However, just when it seemed success was in easy reach, strange things started happening.

Spirit bottles behind the bar would suddenly burst, spraying their contents over seated bar customers. On one occasion a guest staying in an upstairs room complained angrily in the morning about the night-long moaning, groaning and shuffling about next door, despite repeated knocks on the wall and exasperated calls for silence. The landlord looked at him with a bewildered expression before declaring, 'But that room was empty last night!'

The old guys playing draughts in the corner would find pieces suddenly moving by themselves, and beer mugs were moving independently and sliding off tables.

As rumours that the pub was haunted grew, customers started to leave, the business rapidly declined, and the new landlords departed.

Again, after a short time a new young publican and his family moved in, determined to make a go of it. They were far too modern to believe in stories of ghosts and that sort of thing. Again, for a while things went well, and the business was just on the verge of success when the disturbances restarted, this time even more powerfully.

A visitor in the guest room roused the whole house with his shrieks one night, and described how he had awoken to find a dishevelled old woman bending over his bed, a knife in her hands. When he made to push her away she vanished into thin air. Beer mugs started moving rapidly across bars and tables, smashing into each other. Coming down in the morning the landlady would find the furniture re-arranged. This couple also left abruptly.

There have been a dozen landlords since the time of Herbert Langton, and the pub has now been closed for ever, all because of the curse of Lizzie Langton.

THE COACHMAN

Before the carriage road was built in 1758, the coach that ran twice a week between Dorchester and Exeter, unable to enter the town centre, would stop and wait up on the Roman Road at the medieval bridge named Horn Bridge. On arrival the coachman would blow his horn to let the townsfolk know he was there: hence the name of this ancient bridge.

The winter solstice of 1756 was one of the coldest on record. Late that December evening, two thickly clad figures – William, a pale-faced boy of twelve, and his brother Tom, a tall gangly lad of fourteen – could be seen trudging together through the snow along

the river pathway the short distance up to Horn Bridge. Word had come down that the coach, very late that evening, had just arrived.

The river thundered and roared beside them like some malevolent prehistoric beast, threatening at any moment to overleap its banks. The boys jostled each other and laughed to keep their spirits up, rubbing their hands together and stamping their feet against the icy blizzard. It was time for them both to return to Exeter to continue their apprenticeship with their uncle, a silversmith.

Later, the old lady who lived near Horn Bridge confirmed that she had seen the two boys get on the coach that night, but insisted, 'It weren't the usual two-horse carriage. It were four huge black'uns snorting and stamping, like nothing I never seen before, and I couldn't see the face of the coach driver, it were all covered up. Another funny thing, the door just seemed to open of itself. I saw the two lads jump in alright, and the door slammed and the coach went off at a heck of a pace. I could see sparks shooting up from those horses' ooves!' The details became more dramatic with each telling over the following weeks and months.

When no word came from the boys after a week, the family weren't too worried. They assumed things were going well and they would hear from them both soon. However, when a message arrived from the uncle querying their non-arrival on the appointed day, the family approached the coachman and asked him if he remembered taking those two lads.

'What day was zat?' he asked.

When given the date, the old man, rubbing the side of his heavily whiskered face a moment, looked puzzled, then said in his distinct Dorset brogue: 'Oooh no, we never cum through Lyme that day. It were day of the great storm. We broke a wheel and had to stay overnight in Charmouth and change the wheel in the mornin'. There weren't no carriage through Lyme that night!'

Enquiries were made throughout Lyme and Exeter by the distraught parents, but the two boys were never seen nor heard of again.

From that time onwards, any stranger who wished to take the coach to Exeter would be warned by local people:

'Make sure you see the face of the carriage driver before you get on that coach, and you ask him his name!'

LASSIE

The year was 1915, the second year of the First World War. It was a bitterly cold January night when a single lifeboat beached on the shore just below Cobb Gate. Word spread quickly as the extent of the tragedy that had occurred off Portland Bill the day before became known.

HMS Formidable, one of the largest battleships in the fleet, had been sunk by a German U-boat with a loss of over five hundred lives. After many hours tossed about in rough seas, the wet and freezing survivors were in terrible condition and were mostly carried up to the Assembly Rooms, where they were given all the help and medical care that could be provided. The less fortunate ones who had not survived were taken to the Pilot Boat, where their bodies were laid out in the cellar below.

Unnoticed in the confusion, the family dog, Lassie – a crossbreed collie – went down to the cellar and started sniffing those dead sailors. Eventually she settled down by one man and started licking his face. Someone who happened to be passing was startled to see a hand come up to push the dog away, and yelled out 'He's alive!'

Able Seaman John Cohen, upon receiving the assistance he required, survived. He got married, and so far as we know lived happily ever after. He was certainly a great fan of Lassie, the Atkins' dog, who had saved his life. Lassie herself received a medal from the War Office. News reports and photos of the incident can all be seen today in the Pilot Boat and Lyme Regis Museum.

Thus far the story is well known… but that wasn't the end of it. Some time later, Lassie, this much-loved celebrity dog, died. Shortly after, still mourning the loss of his pet, the landlord became aware of a howling in the night coming from the cellar below. Puzzled and uneasy, thinking perhaps a stray dog had somehow got in, he went down to the cellar to investigate, but found nothing.

Thereafter, however, the howling continued intermittently, until they got a new dog in the Pilot Boat. In the course of time this dog also died and the howling recommenced in the cellar.

It was then that the landlord realised, 'Of course! This must be Lassie come back, in case there is another shipwrecked sailor who needs her help, and she only feels it's safe to leave when there is another dog in the Pilot Boat!'

From that time onwards, they have always kept dogs in the Pilot Boat.

THE HOLIDAY LET

'I'll start taking stuff in,' he said as the car stopped at the old cottage. Moments later, with a startled expression, 'Hey Jan, there's someone here!'

'What! Who?

'An old lady, upstairs – must be a mix-up. You sure we've got the right date?'

'Pass me the phone… Hey, Danni? Yes, it's us. No, everything isn't ok! Someone else is here… What? Jan, call the police!'

'Mike, no, wait! I'm going up to talk to her.'

'Excuse me, there must be some mist…' Her throat clamped shut as the old lady in black closed her book, gently rose, and drifted through the adjacent wall…